WINNING BRIDGE
INTANGIBLES

by Mike Lawrence
and Keith Hanson

**Published by
Devyn Press
Louisville, Kentucky**

Cover by Bonnie Baron Pollack

Introduction

In every team sport, one hears frequent references to the "intangibles" of that particular sport. Such attributes as teamwork, fighting spirit, concentration, and hustle will often have more impact on victory or defeat than pure athletic ability. Bridge is a team competition. The "intangibles" of bridge are probably more vital than the intangibles of any sport.

This book does not concern itself with technical bridge skills. The purpose of this book is to help every bridge player to become a winner at the table with the skills he already has.

Printed in the United States of America.

Devyn Press
151 Thierman Lane
Louisville, KY 40207

ISBN 0-910791-15-5

Table of Contents

1. Be a Good Partner

Dealer: North
Vulnerable: North - South

```
                    ♠ —
                    ♡ K Q J 7 3 2
                    ◇ Q J 10
                    ♣ 8 6 5 4
    ♠ A 9                          ♠ K Q 10 7 6 4 3
    ♡ 8 5 4                        ♡ —
    ◇ A 2                          ◇ K 8 7 6 5 3
    ♣ A K Q J 10 3                 ♣ —
                    ♠ J 8 5 2
                    ♡ A 10 9 6
                    ◇ 9 4
                    ♣ 9 7 2
```

North	East	South	West
Jais	Forquet	Trezel	Siniscalco
(France)	(Italy)	(France)	(Italy)
1 ♡	4 ♠	Pass	4 NT
Pass	6 ◇	Pass	6 ♠
Pass	7 ♠	Double	7 NT!
Double	Pass	Pass	Pass

1957 European Championships. Italy vs. France

Trezel's double of 7♠ betrayed the trump position and gave Forquet a chance to make the contract. Siniscalco ran to 7 NT, was doubled and lost the first six heart tricks. Sinascalco's judgment error cost 2870 points!

Italy was still able to recover and win the match due largely to Pietro Forquet. He did not say a word. He removed the previous board from the table and replaced it

4

with the next hand. His good temper enabled Siniscalco to recover his composure and play well the rest of the match.

Analysis:

Pietro Forquet's deportment when this critical disaster occurred helps explain why he has done well at the top levels of bridge for over 25 years. **The most important single skill any bridge player can cultivate is to be a good partner.**

You will bring out the best in your partner by treating him/her with respect and understanding. A smiling and enthusiastic countenance across the table will allow your partners to play their best.

Howard Schenken was a bridge luminary for decades. In the rubber bridge clubs he frequented many players were anxious to play at his table. When queried as to why they wished to play at the table of such a strong player, the typical reply was that they had a big edge as Howard's favorite partner. Each of his "favorite partners" played their best game when they were his partner.

TO REPEAT: THE MOST IMPORTANT SINGLE SKILL ANY BRIDGE PLAYER CAN POSSESS IS TO BE A GOOD PARTNER.

2. Show No Emotion When the Dummy Appears

Dealer: East
Vulnerable: North - South

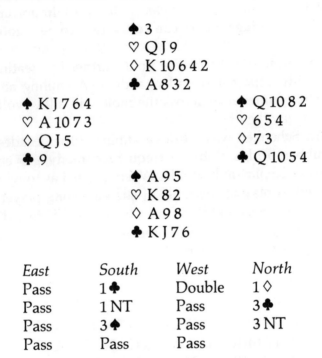

```
                    ♠ 3
                    ♡ Q J 9
                    ◊ K 10 6 4 2
                    ♣ A 8 3 2
    ♠ K J 7 6 4                    ♠ Q 10 8 2
    ♡ A 10 7 3                     ♡ 6 5 4
    ◊ Q J 5                        ◊ 7 3
    ♣ 9                            ♣ Q 10 5 4
                    ♠ A 9 5
                    ♡ K 8 2
                    ◊ A 9 8
                    ♣ K J 7 6
```

East	South	West	North
Pass	1♣	Double	1◊
Pass	1 NT	Pass	3♣
Pass	3♠	Pass	3 NT
Pass	Pass	Pass	

World Championship 1976. North America vs. Italy

North-South bid ambitiously to 3 NT. West led his fourth highest spade to East's queen and declarer's ace. Declarer now played the ace, king, and another diamond to West's queen. West laid down the spade king on which East played the ten. After considerable thought, West underled his spade jack to the declarer's nine! Declarer now made nine tricks and his contract.

Analysis:

The critical time in the play of most bridge hands is the first two or three tricks. The defenders often have available only vague information and must act on inferences and guesswork. As declarer, it is imperative that you don't give them information about whether you are pleased or unhappy with the dummy or the contract by your facial expressions or your attitude.

If the defenders note that you are extremely unhappy, they can draw inferences about what card(s) their partner might possess. Showing pleasure may enable the defenders to cash out and hold you to the minimum number of tricks (most important in duplicate bridge).

An unhappy expression can also take its toll on partner. Partner will not know what you are displeased about and this could cause him needless anxiety.

Many contracts have been salvaged by the declarer who gives no indication of being in dire straits. When your partner has bid madly on his "tram tickets," wait until after the hand to inform him.

SHOW NO EMOTION WHEN DUMMY APPEARS

3. Detach Your Emotions From Previous Hands

Dealer: South
Vulnerable: North - South

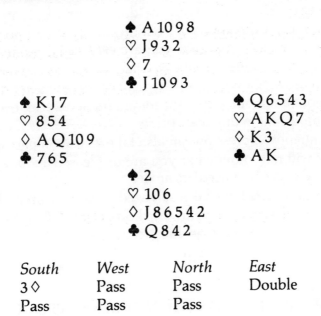

♠ A 10 9 8
♡ J 9 3 2
◊ 7
♣ J 10 9 3

♠ K J 7
♡ 8 5 4
◊ A Q 10 9
♣ 7 6 5

♠ Q 6 5 4 3
♡ A K Q 7
◊ K 3
♣ A K

♠ 2
♡ 10 6
◊ J 8 6 5 4 2
♣ Q 8 4 2

South	West	North	East
3 ◊	Pass	Pass	Double
Pass	Pass	Pass	

South was a player who "steamed" after a "fix" on a preceding hand. Determined to "even the score," he wildly preempted with 3 ◊. He was quickly defeated four tricks doubled for 1100 points to East-West. Many pairs in the duplicate field bid 6♠ and went down. A normal pass would give North-South a chance for a reasonable result.

Analysis:

Successful bridge players approach each new hand having detached themselves from the previous deals.

It can be difficult to think rationally after having made a silly mistake or suffered a disaster of some sort on the previous hand. What often happens is the player then makes an undisciplined bid or play on the present hand.

Pleasure from a good bid, play or result may lead to inadequate attention to the next hand. Inward (hopefully inward) gloating can result in poor concentration on the present hand.

Some players will make wild, unsound bids after a poor result in an attempt to create "action." The usual result is another poor score for the perpetrator of the bid. Every bridge player will have plus and minus positions. All bridge players will make mistakes. All bridge players can achieve better results by not rising too high with the euphoria of success or sinking too low in the flames of failure.

DETACH YOUR EMOTIONS FROM PREVIOUS HANDS

4. Think and Plan at Trick One

Dealer: West
Vulnerable: East - West

```
                    ♠ A 6
                    ♡ A K 7 2
                    ◊ A 8 3 2
                    ♣ 8 4 3
  ♠ Q 10 8 5 2                      ♠ 9 7 3
  ♡ 8 6 5                           ♡ Q J 10 9
  ◊ K J 7 6                         ◊ Q 10 9
  ♣ 5                               ♣ A 9 2
                    ♠ K J 4
                    ♡ 4 3
                    ◊ 5 4
                    ♣ K Q J 10 7 6
```

West	North	East	South
Pass	1◊	Pass	2♣
Pass	2♡	Pass	2 NT
Pass	3 NT	Pass	Pass
Pass			

West led the spade five against 3 NT. Declarer quickly saw the opportunity for a "free finesse" and allowed the trick to run to his jack.

He then leaned forward and began to think, but it was already too late. East held up his club ace until the third round. On the second club trick West discarded the queen of spades to indicate no future in that suit for the defenders. South had no entry to his established club suit and was set two tricks.

South has 10 easy tricks if he simply puts up the spade ace at trick one and plays clubs.

Analysis:

The crucial error on many hands is hasty play to trick one. A good habit to develop as both declarer and defender is to pause briefly before playing to the first trick. Analyze the lead and review the bidding. Make a plan of some sort. Any plan is better than no plan at all.

You can even help your partner develop this habit. As dummy lay the dummy cards leisurely on the table with the suit led placed on the table last. An additional hint: if your partnership has bid a suit during the auction and the contract is now notrump, never place that suit on his left where partner might misconstrue it as trumps.

Many players will make careless, hasty plays early — then agonize when problems develop. Careful play early will often save self-torture later.

THINK AND PLAN AT TRICK ONE

5. Bid and Play in an Even Tempo

Dealer: North
Vulnerable: East - West

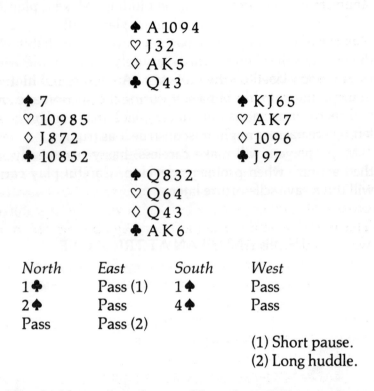

```
                    ♠ A 10 9 4
                    ♡ J 3 2
                    ◇ A K 5
                    ♣ Q 4 3
♠ 7                                 ♠ K J 6 5
♡ 10 9 8 5                          ♡ A K 7
◇ J 8 7 2                           ◇ 10 9 6
♣ 10 8 5 2                          ♣ J 9 7
                    ♠ Q 8 3 2
                    ♡ Q 6 4
                    ◇ Q 4 3
                    ♣ A K 6
```

North	East	South	West
1♣	Pass (1)	1♠	Pass
2♠	Pass	4♠	Pass
Pass	Pass (2)		

(1) Short pause.
(2) Long huddle.

The bidding was direct although 3 NT is a better contract. Perhaps South sould have suggested a notrump contract by bidding 3 NT over North's 2♠ bid. North would have been happy to pass with his flat distribution.

West led the heart ten. East played ace, king and another heart. The correct trump technique now is to play West for one of the trump honors. Normally South would lead a low spade and finesse the ten losing to the jack. Later he would lose a trick to the spade king. South, however, was an expert and had excellent table awareness. Why had a vulnerable East paused noticeably over the 4♠ bid? South drew the correct conclusion that East was considering doubling the final contract. He made the anti-percentage play of ace and another spade to land the contract.

Analysis:

A worthy goal to strive for is to give no information to the opponents by the tempo of your bidding and/or play.

The most effective bridge players bid and play in an even, calm tempo. The best technique is to take a very brief pause before acting in any bidding or play situation. A short pause is not a long huddle but will give you time to think without revealing vital information to an observant opponent when you do have a slight problem. This is not necessary in some extremely obvious situations where your action is fairly routine.

This tip is particularly relevant if you are playing against experts. Evenness in tempo will never be perfectly achieved but is worth striving for.

Playing in tempo and bidding in an even voice will also make you a more ethical player than:
1. The loud quick doubler
2. The fast passer with a terrible hand
3. The slow passer with a moderate hand.

BID AND PLAY IN AN EVEN TEMPO

6. Concentrate Properly

Dealer: South
Vulnerable: East - West
Opening Lead: ♠Q

<pre>
                    ♠ A 8 2
                    ♡ K 8 4 2
                    ◇ A J 10 9
                    ♣ 7 6
    ♠ Q J 10 7 5   ♠ 9 4 3
    ♡ 7 5   ♡ 10 9 3
    ◇ 6 5 4   ◇ K Q 8
    ♣ J 9 8   ♣ K Q 10 2
                    ♠ K 6
                    ♡ A Q J 6
                    ◇ 7 3 2
                    ♣ A 5 4 3
</pre>

North	East	South	West
		1♣	Pass
1◇	Pass	1♡	Pass
2♡	Pass	4♡	Pass
Pass	Pass		

Declarer won the opening spade lead with the king. He led a diamond to the nine losing to the king. A spade return was won by the ace in dummy. Declarer then played four rounds of hearts ending in his hand. He finessed another diamond, the ten losing to the queen and a grateful East-West cashed three spade tricks to put the contract down two.

What was the explanation for this strange declarer play? It was 11 p.m. on the third day of a tournament. Declarer was tired and thought he was playing a contract of 3 NT.

Analysis:

The ability to concentrate is a vital bridge attribute. We all are limited as to how much intense concentration we can muster when applying ourselves to any task. A secret of playing well is not to be "wound up" all session long. Concentrate only when you need to.

Several ways players can conserve concentrative energy are:

1. As dummy, relax and perform dummy's simple duties. Do not scrutinize everyone's play or fret about the fate of the contract.
2. Incessant rehashing of hands between hands or rounds is counter-productive and energy consuming.
3. When playing in a tournament, relax and recharge between sessions. Meticulous examination of every bid and play of the previous session only serves to wear one down. This is especially important in a long tournament.

Bridge players and partnerships improve by "going over" the hands. Do this in moderation at tournaments and not at the table (it's bad manners).

CONCENTRATE PROPERLY

7. Protect Your Cards

Dealer: West
Vulnerable: East - West

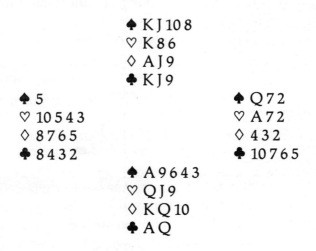

```
              ♠ K J 10 8
              ♡ K 8 6
              ◇ A J 9
              ♣ K J 9
  ♠ 5                      ♠ Q 7 2
  ♡ 10 5 4 3               ♡ A 7 2
  ◇ 8 7 6 5                ◇ 4 3 2
  ♣ 8 4 3 2                ♣ 10 7 6 5
              ♠ A 9 6 4 3
              ♡ Q J 9
              ◇ K Q 10
              ♣ A Q
```

Joe has taken up bridge quite seriously recently. He plays duplicate two or three times a week as well as in the church group he and his wife have always played in. He is working hard at improving his game. Joe was sitting East when this hand came up recently at the club duplicate.

The opponents rolled into 6 spades and West led the heart three. Joe won his ace and returned a heart. The declarer then played a spade to the king and returned the jack. Joe followed low smoothly but the declarer allowed it to ride. 6♠ made was a bottom score for Joe. South had seen Joe's hand and taken an anti-percentage line of play to land the contract.

Analysis:

Bridge is a tough game to play well. The first step towards playing well and achieving reasonable results is to protect your hand from being seen. A large percentage of bridge players will at least occasionally flash their hand to the opponents. Make a conscious effort to guard against your cards being seen by the enemy.

Some hints to accomplish this are:

1. As you pick up your cards and sort them, hold your cards well back.
2. Put singletons and doubletons towards the middle of your hand.
3. Hold your cards straight up and down, not slanted.
4. Keep honors towards the center of your hand and spot cards on the ends.
5. Ask your bridge playing friends if they can ever glimpse your hand.

This point cannot be overemphasized. Hold your hand up and back!

PROTECT YOUR CARDS

8. Do Not Be Intimidated

Dealer: South
Vulnerable: North - South

```
                    ♠ 8 5 2
                    ♡ J 9 6
                    ◇ A 10 3 2
                    ♣ A 6 4
    ♠ J 9                        ♠ Q 7 4
    ♡ A 10 8 2                   ♡ K 7 5 3
    ◇ Q J 4                      ◇ 8 7 5
    ♣ K 9 5 3                    ♣ Q 10 2
                    ♠ A K 10 6 3
                    ♡ Q 4
                    ◇ K 9 6
                    ♣ J 8 7
```

South	West	North	East
1♠	Pass	2♠	Pass
Pass	Double	Pass	3♡
Pass	Pass	Double	

Barb and Peg were playing in their yearly big regional tournament. They elbowed their way through the crowd of kibitzers around the national experts. They had two boards to play. On the first board they bid accurately to a slam that made when a finesse worked.

On the second board, Barb, sitting North, had a maximum raise of Peg's 1♠ opening bid. When expert West doubled and expert East bid 3♡, she had to make a delicate decision. Pass, 3♠ and double were all possibilities. Pass seemed wrong because her side clearly had the majority of HCP and a known fit. If the opponents made 3♡ she would get a poor score; 3♠ seemed like a

18

poor choice with her flat distribution and defensive values. It appeared unlikely that the opponents could made 3♡, so she doubled. During the play Barb and Peg took two spades, two diamonds, a heart and a club for +300 and a near top. If Barb had been intimidated into a pass by her expert opponents, she would have been +100. It would not have been enough to compensate her for the +110 available in 2♠, and would have resulted in a below average score.

Analysis:

Bridge provides the opportunity to improve by competing against better players. Bridge players can enter tournaments and compete against the top experts in the game. This is a unique opportunity in competitive activities. Golfers cannot play golf against Nicklaus and tennis players cannot play tennis against Navratilova. Bridge players can sit down and complete with world and national champions.

The key in competing against good players, whether they are the best in the world or the best at your club, is poise. The player who is intimidated by the expert will be easy prey.

Aces and kings will take tricks against anyone. Experts will occasionally be ruffled as they wonder why you are not intimidated when you play at their table.

So compete with confidence against everyone. Good results can often be achieved by keeping your wits about you.

DO NOT BE INTIMIDATED

9. Be a Tough Competitor

Dealer: North
Vulnerable: North - South

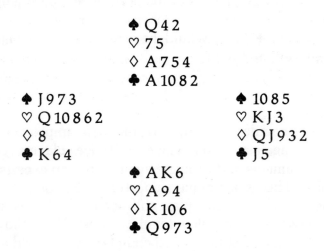

```
              ♠ Q 4 2
              ♡ 7 5
              ◇ A 7 5 4
              ♣ A 10 8 2
♠ J 9 7 3                    ♠ 10 8 5
♡ Q 10 8 6 2                 ♡ K J 3
◇ 8                          ◇ Q J 9 3 2
♣ K 6 4                      ♣ J 5
              ♠ A K 6
              ♡ A 9 4
              ◇ K 10 6
              ♣ Q 9 7 3
```

Terry and Joyce were five rounds through the duplicate session and were not distinguishing themselves. Joyce declared 3 NT on the above hand and listlessly went down. Before round six, Terry informed Joyce he did not care to play with anyone who did not give a good effort the entire session. Joyce then played intensely the remainder of the session and they salvaged fifth place after their poor start. Terry was the best competitor at his club and it rubbed off on his partners.

Joyce went down in 3 NT after she held up the heart ace until the third round. She then sloppily led a small club to the ace and a club back. West took his king and cashed his two heart tricks for down one. She only needed to take a double club finesse to land her game.

Analysis:

Bridge is a difficult game. There will be inevitable poor sessions because of the variables with the cards, judgment, partnership and system. When those sessions occur, the truly tough players retain their equilibrium and continue trying.

A leading world champion player has stated, "Anyone can play well and put forth good effort when events are going smoothly. The trick is to hang tough, not become demoralized, and play as well as possible when the session is going poorly."

The result of a few inferior scores is often subsequent disasters for many players as they become inattentive and careless. You can earn partner's gratitude by hanging tough. He is then likely to do the same for you.

BE A TOUGH COMPETITOR

10. Act Decisively — Achieve a Reputation

DEALER: North
VULNERABLE: North - South

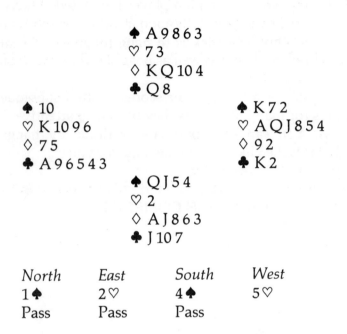

```
                    ♠ A 9 8 6 3
                    ♡ 7 3
                    ◇ K Q 10 4
                    ♣ Q 8
    ♠ 10                              ♠ K 7 2
    ♡ K 10 9 6                        ♡ A Q J 8 5 4
    ◇ 7 5                             ◇ 9 2
    ♣ A 9 6 5 4 3                     ♣ K 2
                    ♠ Q J 5 4
                    ♡ 2
                    ◇ A J 8 6 3
                    ♣ J 10 7
```

North	East	South	West
1♠	2♡	4♠	5♡
Pass	Pass	Pass	

In a matchpoint game, North opened a light 1♠ and East overcalled 2♡. South bid a direct 4♠. West now had a difficult decision and decided to bid 5♡. All passed and a spade lead to the ace and diamond switch netted the defenders the first three tricks for down one. Most of the field was allowed to play 4♡ making, or were doubling 4♠ for down one on a slower auction. South's bold 4♠ bid reaped the reward of a fine score on the board.

Analysis:

Conduct yourself in a confident and positive manner at the bridge table. The proper method of reflecting decisiveness is to give the matter proper thought and then act as if you know what you are doing.

Table habits to have:

1.   Be attentive and alert during the auction so you needn't ask for frequent reviews of the bidding.
2.   Consider mentally your proper play and then proceed confidently without hesitantly detaching and replacing cards.
3.   Bid firmly. Tenuous or doubtful bidding attracts doubles that firm bidding does not.

Bridge is a partnership game. A positive manner will enhance your ability to attract a better partner. This will improve your scores and bolster your reputation. A firm table presence will give your partner confidence in you and impress your opponents.

One additional point — keep your mouth closed unless you are absolutely sure you know what you are talking about.

ACT DECISIVELY — ACHIEVE A REPUTATION

11. The More Experienced Partner Should Adapt

Dealer: South
Vulnerable: East - West

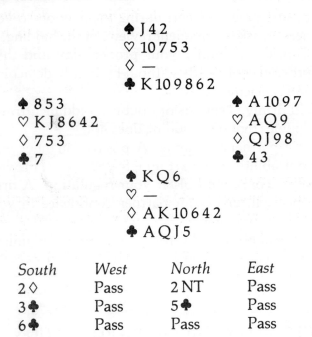

```
                    ♠ J 4 2
                    ♡ 10 7 5 3
                    ◊ —
                    ♣ K 10 9 8 6 2
  ♠ 8 5 3                          ♠ A 10 9 7
  ♡ K J 8 6 4 2                    ♡ A Q 9
  ◊ 7 5 3                          ◊ Q J 9 8
  ♣ 7                              ♣ 4 3
                    ♠ K Q 6
                    ♡ —
                    ◊ A K 10 6 4 2
                    ♣ A Q J 5
```

South	West	North	East
2 ◊	Pass	2 NT	Pass
3 ♣	Pass	5 ♣	Pass
6 ♣	Pass	Pass	Pass

South is the most experienced player in his club. He is respected for his ability to obtain good results playing with many different and unfamiliar partners.

South preferred weak two bids. North was only familiar with strong two bids; South readily agreed to play them. Strong two bids facilitated a smooth auction to 6♣ and a top score for North - South on the above deal. At several other tables South opened the hand one diamond and was passed out!

The above hand illustrates that simple, well-understood

24

methods work efficiently on most deals. To be comfortable with the bidding system is more important than the actual agreements used.

Analysis:

Partnerships are often unequal in their level of bridge experience and familiarity with conventions. It behooves the more experienced player to adapt his game to his partner.

As the more experienced player:

1. Agree to play a basic bidding system so your partner will feel at ease.
2. Play familiar leads and signals that are easy to remember.
3. Avoid making confusing or obscure bids to demonstrate your bridge "expertise."

Successful professional bridge players are noteworthy for their ability to adapt. They must adjust to achieve good results with a variety of less expert partners. They especially will not burden partners with cumbersome or unfamiliar conventions.

Be adaptive in a pleasant, friendly manner. Results may still be poor if a condescending, superior attitude is demonstrated.

THE MORE EXPERIENCED PARTNER
SHOULD ADAPT

12. Adhere to Your System

Dealer: South
Vulnerable: None

<pre>
                    ♠ K 8 7
                    ♡ A Q J
                    ◇ K J 8
                    ♣ K J 4 2
  ♠ A 5 3 2   ♠ 10 6 4
  ♡ 9 8 6 3   ♡ 7 5 4 2
  ◇ A 7   ◇ 9 6 5
  ♣ 9 7 3   ♣ 10 6 5
                    ♠ Q J 9
                    ♡ K 10
                    ◇ Q 10 4 3 2
                    ♣ A Q 8
</pre>

South	West	North	East
1 NT (1)	Pass	6 NT	Pass
Pass	Double	Pass	Pass
Pass			

(1) 15-17 HCP

South was a player who liked to turn bridge into a guessing game. He loved to mastermind at the table. On the hand above, after South opened 1 NT, North knew that his side could not be missing an AK in any suit (he was looking at the ace or king in every suit) nor could they be missing two aces. He had 18 HCP and even if South had the minimum of 15 HCP that he promised, the partnership had 33 HCP. So the opponents could not have the 8 HCP necessary to hold two aces and North bid a direct 6 NT.

South is running out of partners.

Analysis:

Bridge is a game where partners make certain agreements regarding the bidding system they will follow.

To achieve best results, both partners must adhere to this system.

Common anti-system violations are:

1. Deliberately passing partner's forcing bid because of a feeling of having previously overbid.

2. Making a bid with either insufficient or excessive values as defined within the partnership. The most frequent examples of this type of violation are opening 1 NT with less HCP than the minimum or more HCP than the maximum; opening a weak two bid with less HCP than the minimum; opening one of a suit with insufficient values; responding one of a suit or raising partner's suit with less than 6 points; and overcalling with insufficient values.

3. Lying about the number of aces in response to a Blackwood bid.

A system violation is intentionally taking an anti-system action because of your "intuition" or fear. Partnership trust is vital to good bridge. Stick to your bidding system so your partner can trust you.

ADHERE TO YOUR SYSTEM

13. Be Selective in Using Conventions

Dealer: North
Vulnerable: North - South

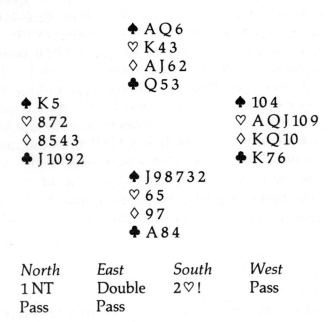

```
              ♠ A Q 6
              ♡ K 4 3
              ◊ A J 6 2
              ♣ Q 5 3
♠ K 5                        ♠ 10 4
♡ 8 7 2                      ♡ A Q J 10 9
◊ 8 5 4 3                    ◊ K Q 10
♣ J 10 9 2                   ♣ K 7 6
              ♠ J 9 8 7 3 2
              ♡ 6 5
              ◊ 9 7
              ♣ A 8 4
```

North	East	South	West
1 NT	Double	2 ♡ !	Pass
Pass	Pass		

North was the club's "convention fanatic." He and South were a new partnership. Prior to the game North had insisted on playing many conventions with which his partner had an incomplete understanding. The above hand was early in the evening. They had agreed to use Jacoby Transfer Bids but had not discussed an agreement after interference.

North - South were down three at 2 ♡ instead of making their spade partscore.

Analysis:

Many conventions are excellent and have added to the enjoyment of the game of bridge. Artificial conventions such as Stayman and Blackwood are so popular and common as to be considered "standard."

However, every convention has its price. Every artificial bid you tack on your system will in some way detract from your natural bidding. Therefore, it is necessary to select only conventions that will be assets rather than liabilities.

Use the following guidelines in selecting conventions:
1. Is the convention easy to remember?
2. Do both partners understand and know the follow-up bids to the convention?*
3. Does the convention occur frequently enough to warrant the effort to remember it?
4. Does the convention have technical merit?

An infrequent partnership should keep conventions to a minimum. A player overburdened by conventions will often use his energy memorizing and worrying about conventions rather than putting his concentration to better use in bidding judgment, play and defense.

A nationally renowned player has stated, "Conventions never made a poor player into a good player, but too many conventions have made good players into poor players."

BE SELECTIVE IN USING CONVENTIONS

*Mike Lawrence's *Partnership Understandings* is recommended to solve this problem.

14.
Don't Catch The "New York Times" Syndrome

Dealer: West
Vulnerable: None
Opening Lead: ♣J

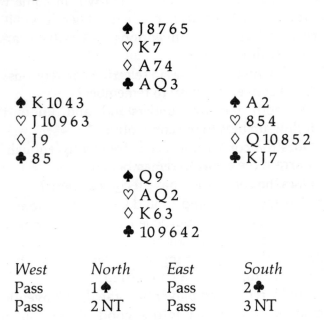

	♠ J8765	
	♡ K7	
	◇ A74	
	♣ AQ3	
♠ K1043		♠ A2
♡ J10963		♡ 854
◇ J9		◇ Q10852
♣ 85		♣ KJ7
	♠ Q9	
	♡ AQ2	
	◇ K63	
	♣ 109642	

West	North	East	South
Pass	1♠	Pass	2♣
Pass	2 NT	Pass	3 NT

In a team match the bidding was the same at both tables. At Table 1, East led a normal diamond and the foul lie of the clubs caused declarer to go down three. At Table 2, East was a good player who had a penchant for the spectacular. He decided the club jack would be a tricky lead. The spectacular result was 3 NT making three!

Analysis:

There is a certain type of player who is constantly snatching at opportunities to be tricky and devious.

Examples of this might be:

1. A very unusual opening lead.
2. Psyching or frequent "tactical" bids.
3. Trap passing or "master-minding" the auction.

A leading East-Coast player was described as having the "New York Times" syndrome. He often attempted to concoct a "brilliant" bid or play that would warrant the hand and his name's inclusion in the *New York Times'* bridge column. As in most competitive activities, the contest is not won by the occasional, erratic brilliancy. The victor is the competitor who plays consistently and steadily with few errors.

There is scope for creativity and flair in bridge. Just don't go to extremes.

DON'T CATCH THE "NEW YORK TIMES" SYNDROME

15. Do Not Lose Interest When Holding a Terrible Hand

Dealer: North
Vulnerable: Both
Opening Lead: ♣2

```
              ♠ A K 4
              ♡ K 9 8
              ◇ Q J 10 8
              ♣ A Q 8
♠ J 7 2                        ♠ 10 9 5 3
♡ Q 7 5 3                      ♡ 4
◇ 5 4 2                        ◇ 9 7 3
♣ 9 7 2                        ♣ J 10 5 4 3
              ♠ Q 8 6
              ♡ A J 10 6 2
              ◇ A K 6
              ♣ K 6
```

North	East	South	West
1◇	Pass	1♡	Pass
2 NT	Pass	3◇	Pass
3♡	Pass	4 NT	Pass
5♡	Pass	5 NT	Pass
6♡	Pass	7♡	Pass
Pass	Pass		

The time was nearing midnight. East was in his tenth consecutive hour of high stakes rubber bridge. The cards had not been kind to him this day and he was a substantial loser. The opponents bid swiftly to 7♡. East groaned and vacantly stared at the ceiling as he calculated the damages of a vulnerable grand slam. This behavior was not lost on South who noticed East's discouraged attitude. He led the heart jack and ran it to land the grand slam.

Analysis:

It is normal human behavior to generate more enthusiasm for good hands than poor hands. It is also quite normal to defend attentively when you see the real likelihood of defeating the contract and not so attentively when the cause looks dim. When a player for the umpteenth time in a session has a poor hand, he must struggle again in the energy-consuming task of defeating the contract.

An astute declarer may succeed in an impossible or difficult contract by noticing the diligence of the opponents. When one defender seems bored, declarer can often play the hand more accurately.

Protect your partner's possible assets and cause declarer the most problems possible.

DO NOT LOSE INTEREST WHEN HOLDING A TERRIBLE HAND

16.
Do Not Teach
During The Session

Dealer: South
Vulnerable: None

```
                    ♠ Q J 4
                    ♡ A 7 5 2
                    ◇ 8 6 3
                    ♣ 8 5 4
    ♠ A 9 7 5                      ♠ K 10 3
    ♡ Q 10 8 3                     ♡ 9 6
    ◇ J 7                          ◇ K Q 5 2
    ♣ 10 9 6 2                     ♣ J 7 3
                    ♠ 8 6 2
                    ♡ K J 4
                    ◇ A 10 9 4
                    ♣ A K Q
```

South	West	North	East
1 ◇	Pass	1 ♡	Pass
3 ♡	Pass	Pass	Pass

North and South were first-time partners at the club. North was a player who enjoyed teaching while the session was in progress. On an earlier hand, South had opened 1 NT with hearts unstopped and gotten a poor result. North now dredged up one of his "rules" which was never to open 1 NT without both major suits securely stopped. When this hand arrived, South felt sure that 1 NT was the proper opening bid. But bowing to partner's wishes, he decided to open 1 ◇. The resulting 3 ♡ contact went down two for a bottom score. 1 NT was making one or two at all the other tables.

Analysis:

Little is accomplished by attempting to teach partner during the session. There are several reasons for this:

1. Most partners feel **they** should be the teacher and won't appreciate instruction.
2. Partner may try too hard to please you and not play his natural game. Confusion will reign as he tries to remember and fit everything together.
3. Instruction cannot be beneficial between hands. Partner will resent being blamed or made the scapegoat in front of his peers.

Not teaching during the session is particularly relevant if playing with a new or infrequent partner.

You and your regular partner(s) may choose to analyze and discuss during the session. This should be done away from the table.

Superior results will be obtained with any partner by relaxing and just playing bridge while the session is in progress.

DO NOT TEACH DURING THE SESSION

17. Develop a Killer Instinct

Dealer: South
Vulnerable: North - South

```
                    ♠ A 5 4 3 2
                    ♡ K J 6
                    ◇ 10 3
                    ♣ K 9 6
♠ —                                ♠ Q J 10 9 7
♡ 10 9 8 7 4 3                     ♡ A 5 2
◇ J 8 4                            ◇ A 7 6
♣ Q J 8 7                          ♣ 4 3
                    ♠ K 8 6
                    ♡ Q
                    ◇ K Q 9 5 2
                    ♣ A 10 5 2
```

South	West	North	East
1◇	Pass	1♠	Pass
2♣	Pass	2 NT	Pass
3♠	Pass	4♠	Pass!
Pass	Pass		

East is a well-mannered player of just over two years bridge experience. His standard of play is improving rapidly. He often places but seldom wins and the above hand illustrates the reason. North - South (East's friends) bid tenuously to 4♠ and all passed. East knew they were receiving bad breaks and should have doubled. Plus 200 for East - West was a below average score while plus 500 was a tie for top.

Analysis:

A baseball saying is "friendship ceases when you step between the white lines." The winning bridge player's motto is "friendship ceases during the hand."

Many players have the attitude that it is improper or uncouth to preempt, sacrifice, double, balance, or in general make life difficult for the opponents. Until that hurdle is crossed, any player's bridge future is severely limited.

Bridge is intended to be a competitive game. Doubles and other maximum score tactics are the very heart and soul of bridge. You can and should be a friendly, courteous competitor both at and away from the table.

But while the hand is in progress —

DEVELOP A KILLER INSTINCT

18. Develop a Positive Mental Attitude

Dealer: South
Vulnerable: None
Opening Lead: ♡6

```
                    ♠ K 7 6
                    ♡ 7 4
                    ◇ A K 5
                    ♣ J 10 5 4 2
     ♠ 10 9 8                      ♠ Q 4 2
     ♡ K Q 8 6 2                   ♡ J 9 5 3
     ◇ Q 7 6                       ◇ 9 8 3
     ♣ 9 6                         ♣ A 8 7
                    ♠ A J 5 3
                    ♡ A 10
                    ◇ J 10 4 2
                    ♣ K Q 3
```

Southwas the number one pessimist in the rubber bridge game. To any and all who would listen, he hastened to relate that "nothing ever works for me." Declaring the above hand after the heart lead, he realized he needed a 3-3 spade break with the queen onside and the same luck in diamonds to make his 3 NT contract. He resignedly conceded a club and was swiftly down one. His contract was actually there for the taking. (In duplicate bridge, South's play was correct. At rubber bridge or teams, South should go all out for success. He had failed to evaluate his contract correctly — see page 46).

Analysis:

"I never get any breaks."
"My finesses always lose."
"Another fix."
"I never get any cards."
Familiar refrains by many bridge players.

The truth is that over the long haul every bridge player will win just as many finesses, receive the same number of good and bad breaks, hold the same number of excellent and poor hands, and be "fixed" no more than anyone else.

A pessimistic approach is a distinct handicap to success in any endeavor. Contestants are often relatively equal in ability. A player who acts in a confident and positive manner will win more often than his skill alone would warrant.

DEVELOP A POSITIVE MENTAL ATTITUDE

19. Strive To Improve

Dealer: South
Vulnerable: East - West
Opening Lead: ♠2

```
                    ♠ 8
                    ♡ Q65
                    ◊ AQ83
                    ♣ KJ1042
  ♠ KJ952                        ♠ AQ7643
  ♡ 1087                         ♡ 942
  ◊ 542                          ◊ 106
  ♣ 87                           ♣ Q6
                    ♠ 10
                    ♡ AKJ3
                    ◊ KJ97
                    ♣ A953
```

South	West	North	East
1◊	Pass	3◊	Pass
3♡	Pass	4♣	Pass
4NT	Pass	5◊	Pass
6◊	Pass	Pass	Pass

South was a very good player who had been successful for many years. After the lead of the deuce of spades, he won the heart return, drew trumps, cashed all his hearts (discarding a club from dummy) and stopped to count the distribution of the hand. West was known to have three hearts and three diamonds. In addition South counted West to have four spades because of the opening lead of the spade deuce. This would leave West with three clubs. Confidently South cashed the ace of clubs and, when all played low, led a low club to dummy's jack and

East's queen.

South was stunned.

Although an expert, he had become lackadaisical about keeping abreast of modern developments in the game. Consequently no bell went off to look at the opponents' convention card after the opening lead. If he had looked he would have discovered that the opponents lead their lowest card from a three or five card suit, but third highest from a four card suit. Thus he would have known that West had five spades, three hearts, three diamonds and therefore two clubs, and the queen of clubs must drop if the ace and king were played.

It is apparent that even an expert (as demonstrated by his play of the hand) must continue to learn or he will lose his effectiveness.

Analysis:

At a recent ACBL National Tournament panel show, a two-time World Champion player with over 10,000 master points was asked this question, "What goals can a player of your lofty status possibly work for when you have already accomplished so much?" The answer was "I just hope to continue working on improving my game."

Striving for improvement is essential for players at each level of the game. You need not devote an enormous number of hours a week in this pursuit.

Simply recognizing that you have room for growth and the willingness to learn are the keys. Probably the easiest and most desirable methods of improving are to:

1. Ask questions of better players.
2. Read worthwhile bridge books.
3. Participate with and against the strongest players possible.

The game will be more stimulating and interesting if you

STRIVE TO IMPROVE

41

20. Analyze Objectively

DEALER: North
VULNERABLE: North-South
OPENING LEAD: ♡9

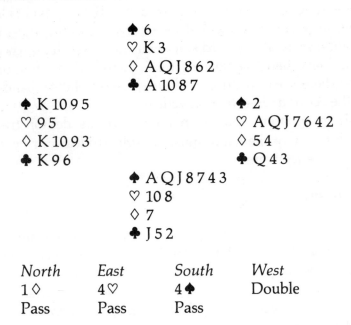

	North	♠ 6	
		♡ K 3	
		◊ A Q J 8 6 2	
		♣ A 10 8 7	

♠ K 10 9 5   ♠ 2
♡ 9 5   ♡ A Q J 7 6 4 2
◊ K 10 9 3   ◊ 5 4
♣ K 9 6   ♣ Q 4 3

♠ A Q J 8 7 4 3
♡ 10 8
◊ 7
♣ J 5 2

North	East	South	West
1 ◊	4 ♡	4 ♠	Double
Pass	Pass	Pass	

South was an enthusiastic player with only one year of tournament experience.

After East's 4♡ preempt, South made the normal bid of 4♠. West doubled and South was down two for a loss of 500 points.

South's husband, sitting North, snarled "What made you think you should bid vulnerable at the four-level with only eight high card points? They were going down in 4♡."

South was apologetic and felt she had made a horrible error. She will have a difficult time in her development as a bridge player because of the illogical and unobjective analysis presented as a model by her husband.

Analysis:

Bridge players grow by analyzing the hands.

It is crucial that this analysis be objective. Do not look at the result of the actual hand. A completely correct bid, lead or play may have worked out poorly. A lunatic action may occasionally find a pot of gold. Do not fall into the trap of labelling a normal action that results in a poor score as a mistake. On the other hand, mistakes should be examined even when they resulted in a good score.

A player's technical skills and confidence will develop best if the post-mortem analysis is accurate, unemotional and objective.

ANALYZE OBJECTIVELY

21. Develop a Bridge Sense of Humor

DEALER: South
VULNERABLE: East-West
OPENING LEAD: ♣9

```
                    ♠ J 10 8 5 2
                    ♡ K 10
                    ◊ K 10 4
                    ♣ A K 6
  ♠ —                              ♠ K Q 9 7 6 4 3
  ♡ 6 3 2                          ♡ 7 5
  ◊ A J 7 6                        ◊ 9 5 2
  ♣ 9 8 7 4 3 2                    ♣ 5
                    ♠ A
                    ♡ A Q J 9 8 4
                    ◊ Q 8 3
                    ♣ Q J 10
```

North	East	South	West
—	—	1♡	Pass
1♠	Pass	3♡	Pass
4♣	Pass	4♠	Pass
6♡	Pass	Pass	Pass

After North - South aggresively bid to 6♡, West led the seven of clubs. South decided to try to establish dummy's fifth spade rather than rely solely on the diamond finesse. Consequently he won the opening club lead in his hand and laid down the ace of spades. South was horrified when West ruffed. Pragmatically, West cashed the ace of diamonds before giving his partner a club ruff for down two. South was still in a state of shock. North, with a twinkle in his eye, asked "Are you sure you took the best line of play?"

North - South are a very successful partnership that has lasted for more than 20 years. Their achievements are due in no small part to their ability to laugh at themselves.

Analysis:

The game of bridge lends itself to many humorous situations and to many more situations where you want to either laugh, cry or scream. It's always best to laugh. When a ludicrous result occurs (as inevitably happens), relax and enjoy the humor in the situation.

Intense concentration and a fiery competitive spirit are needed to play bridge well. However, the ability to accept the game's injustices and partner's fallacies with a degree of humor will enable you to get the best game from partner in the current session, to play the best that you can and to maintain a long-standing, successful partnership.

Enjoy the lighter side of the game.

DEVELOP A BRIDGE SENSE OF HUMOR

22. Evaluate Your Contract

DEALER: South
VULNERABLE: None
OPENING LEAD: ♠ 10

```
                    ♠ 6 5
                    ♡ J 10 6 4 3
                    ◇ K J
                    ♣ K 8 6 5
    ♠ 10 9 8 7 3                    ♠ K Q J 2
    ♡ 7                             ♡ 9 8
    ◇ Q 8 4 2                       ◇ 10 9 5 3
    ♣ J 9 7                         ♣ Q 10 3
                    ♠ A 4
                    ♡ A K Q 5 2
                    ◇ A 7 6
                    ♣ A 4 2
```

North	East	South	West
—	—	2 NT	Pass
3 NT	Pass	Pass	Pass

Declarer paused before playing to trick one. His choice of opening bids and his partner's strange decision to suppress his five-card heart suit resulted in a 3 NT contract that was unlikely to be duplicated elsewhere in the field.

Declarer realized three things: that the normal 4 ♡ contract would easily make with an overtrick; that he had only ten top tricks in his 3 NT contract; and that 3 NT making four would result in very few, if any, match-points.

Therefore, South took his only reasonable chance for 11 tricks by closing his eyes and leading a diamond to the jack. When he reopened his eyes he had 11 tricks and an excellent duplicate score.

The important thing to understand is that 3 NT going down would have been the same score as 3 NT making four because the field was going to be in 4♡ making five.

Analysis:

Matchpoint scoring is based on a comparison of your score against the other scores in the field. The absolute value of your score is irrelevant. Therefore your goal is not making your contract but to achieve a better score than the other pairs in your section. An evaluation of your contract is often a critical first step in determining how you will declare a hand. Three situations in which contract evaluation is especially important are:

1. **Sacrifices:** You have sacrificed against the opponents' game or slam. You must assume their contract would have been successful and make every effort to hold your losses to less than the value of their contract. You will take any risk to try to hold your losses to this value and conversely you will take any safety plays that will ensure that you won't lose more than this value. For example, let's say that you have bid 4♠ over an opponent's 4♡ contract. They are vulnerable and you are not. You will take any risk to hold your losses to 500 points. If you go down 900 or even 1100 points when you could have held the loss to 700 points, it is almost irrelevant. Your only goal was to take seven tricks. On the other hand if it is probable that you can hold your loss to 300 points but this risks losing 700 points, don't consider this play; take the sure minus 500. The difference between a 300 and 500 point loss is immaterial but the difference between a 500

47

and 700 point loss is critical.

2. **Games:** Your bidding has landed you in an inferior scoring game contract. As in the example hand, you may have to risk your contract in an attempt to draw even or to outscore the other pairs in the field who are in the normal contract.

3. **Partscores:** You must try to estimate what score the opponents could have achieved if they had played the hand. You must try to better this score. For example, if you estimate that the opponents can make 2 ♠, you must limit your loss on the hand to −100. You must be particularly careful to avoid the "kiss of death" score of −200 on partscore hands.

Playing matchpoints, on most hands you will simply try to take as many tricks as possible. However, there are situations when an evaluation of your contract and the probable results at the other tables may lead you to adopt an unorthodox line of play.

EVALUATE YOUR CONTRACT

23. Be a Real Player

Caution: Your bid line has landed you in an in...
...with its complications. As in the example...

DEALER: South
VULNERABLE: None

♠ AQ84
♥ AQJ8
♦ ...
♣ SA...

...Opener... ♦ T80

Interpretation: You may...
use it however it may...
...lity to accept...
...ith a degree...

♣ A9

South	West	North	East
1♥	Pass		
1♠	Pass		
3♣	P...		

South was an excellent player, partnered with a novice. His ♣ cue bid has meant playing with an expert. He may reach an unlikely slam or need help in evaluating what to do if the opponents bid 5♠. However, the cue bid was a bad practical choice, playing with an inexperienced partner. He misunderstood the bid and passed. North-South played 2♦ down three rather than 3♣ making four.

Analysis

S. J. Simon, in his classic book *Why You Lose at Bridge*...

23. Be a Practical Player

DEALER: West
VULNERABLE: None

```
                        ♠ 4 3
                        ♡ A Q J 8 6
                        ◊ K 7 5
                        ♣ 5 4 2
        ♠ Q 10 9                    ♠ K J 8 2
        ♡ 2                         ♡ 7 5
        ◊ A Q J 6                   ◊ 10 9 4 3
        ♣ K J 8 7 6                 ♣ Q 10 3
                        ♠ A 7 6 5
                        ♡ K 10 9 4 3
                        ◊ 8 2
                        ♣ A 9
```

North	East	South	West
—	—	—	1♣
1♡	1♠	2♣	Pass
Pass	Pass		

South was an excellent player partnered with a novice. His 2♣ cue bid has merit playing with an expert: he may reach an unlikely slam or need help in evaluating what to do if the opponents bid 5♣. However, the cue bid was a bad practical choice playing with an inexperienced partner. He misunderstood the bid and passed! North - South played 2♣ down three rather than 4♡ making four.

Analysis:

S. J. Simon, in his classic book, *Why You Lose at Bridge*

described the difference between "the best possible result" and "the best result possible." During the auction or on defense, it will often happen that you can see you might get a perfect result if you can induce your partner to take some particular action. However, if he errs, the result may be disastrous. In those situations, it is usually best to try for "the best result possible" rather than "the best possible result."

Example 1: Defending against a difficult contract, you realize that the hand can be defeated by two tricks if you can induce partner to defend in a precise manner. However, if partner misses this difficult defense, the declarer will make his contract. A second line of defense will always defeat the contract one trick regardless of partner's play but gives up all chance of defeating the contract more than one trick. Go for the one trick set. It is "the best result possible" although not "the best possible result."

Example 2: A noted bridge authority has stated "You can't land on the head of a pin on every hand." The auction is an estimate of the trick-taking potential of the hand. It is not an exact science (no matter how hard some players try to make it so). When the bidding indicates that some contract has a reasonable chance for success, the practical player will just bid what he thinks he can make.

BE A PRACTICAL PLAYER

24. Improve Your Bridge Etiquette

DEALER: South
VULNERABLE: None
OPENING LEAD: ♣Q

```
                    ♠ 10 7 6
                    ♡ Q 10 8
                    ◊ K 6 4
                    ♣ A 7 5 3
      ♠ A Q 5 2                    ♠ K J 9
      ♡ 5 3 2                      ♡ 7 6
      ◊ 5 3                        ◊ J 10 9 7
      ♣ Q J 10 9                   ♣ K 8 6 2
                    ♠ 8 4 3
                    ♡ A K J 9 4
                    ◊ A Q 8 2
                    ♣ 4
```

North	East	South	West
—	—	1♡	Pass
2♡	Pass	3◊	Pass
4♡	Pass	Pass	Pass

West led the queen of clubs against the 4♡ contract. South thought for a long time before she played at trick one. Then she won the ace of clubs, ruffed a club, played a heart to dummy's ten and ruffed another club with the ace of hearts. She then led the heart jack to dummy's queen and ruffed the last club with the king of hearts. A diamond to dummy's king let declarer draw the defender's last trump with the heart eight. The ace and queen of diamonds were declarer's ninth and tenth tricks. West smiled graciously and said, "Nicely played . . . very nicely played."

South was an average player with a keen interest in the game. She was working hard to improve. West was an extremely popular expert, noted not only for his bridge skill, but also for his pleasant demeanor and impeccable manners.

South floated on air for the rest of the session.

Analysis:

All bridge players, but especially more experienced players, should provide an example of good bridge etiquette for others to emulate.

Etiquette Guidelines

1. Be courteous to partner and opponents at **all** times.
2. Avoid remarks or actions that might annoy or embarrass another player.
3. A call for the director should be made, when necessary, in a manner that is courteous to the other players and to the director.
4. Don't take offense at inadvertent or ignorant breaches of etiquette by other players, especially inexperienced ones.
5. Maintain a pleasant demeanor.
6. Refrain from unnecessary talking during a hand or between the boards of a round.
7. Be a good sport. Compliment your partner or the opponents when it is deserved.
8. Avoid gloating after a good result.
9. Avoid griping after a bad result.
10. Abide by the director's decisions with graciousness.

Good bridge etiquette will make you a popular player. Other players will applaud your successes and commiserate with you in your failures.

Bad bridge manners result in an atmosphere of hostility.

When such a player does well, an air of suspicion and detachment surrounds him. Regardless of his ability and results, he will eventually run out of partners and team-mates.

It is in every player's self-interest to develop good bridge etiquette.

IMPROVE YOUR BRIDGE ETIQUETTE

25. Putting It All to Work

About 200 years ago Benjamin Franklin decided to improve his character. Each week he stressed one virtue that he wished to acquire. For example, one week he would concentrate on being frugal. The next week he would focus on avoiding idle gossip. When he finished his long list of self-improvements, he repeated the list many times over. He knew from personal experience that vague attempts to improve several behavior patterns simultaneously would not work.

You, dear reader, should approach this book in the same spirit. Grade yourself on the bridge intangibles listed on the following page. Select those items that you want to change in yourself. Choose **one** behavior that you want to improve. Concentrate on improving that one behavior for your next five sessions. Then choose another area in which you want to improve and concentrate on that for the next five sessions. Proceed down your "Want to Improve" list until you have completed it. Then start at the beginning of the list and repeat the process several times until you have reached the goals you set for yourself.

GOOD LUCK

Intangibles Behavior Checklist

	ALWAYS	USUALLY	SOMETIMES	SELDOM
1. Are you a good partner?	☐	☐	☐	☐
2. Do you show no emotion when dummy appears?	☐	☐	☐	☐
3. Do you detach your emotions from previous hands?	☐	☐	☐	☐
4. Do you think and plan at trick 1?	☐	☐	☐	☐
5. Do you bid and play in an even tempo?	☐	☐	☐	☐
6. Do you concentrate properly?	☐	☐	☐	☐
7. Do you protect your cards?	☐	☐	☐	☐
8. Do you avoid intimidation?	☐	☐	☐	☐
9. Are you a tough competitor?	☐	☐	☐	☐
10. Do you act decisively?	☐	☐	☐	☐
11. Do you adapt to less experienced partners?	☐	☐	☐	☐
12. Do you adhere to your system?	☐	☐	☐	☐
13. Are you selective in using conventions?	☐	☐	☐	☐

	ALWAYS	USUALLY	SOMETIMES	SELDOM
14. Do you avoid "The New York Times Syndrome?"	☐	☐	☐	☐
15. Do you keep interest when holding a terrible hand?	☐	☐	☐	☐
16. Do you avoid teaching during the session?	☐	☐	☐	☐
17. Do you have a killer instinct?	☐	☐	☐	☐
18. Do you have a positive mental attitude?	☐	☐	☐	☐
19. Do you strive to improve?	☐	☐	☐	☐
20. Do you analyze objectively?	☐	☐	☐	☐
21. Do you have a bridge sense of humor?	☐	☐	☐	☐
22. Do you evaluate your contract?	☐	☐	☐	☐
23. Are you a practical player?	☐	☐	☐	☐
24. Do you observe good bridge etiquette?	☐	☐	☐	☐

THE BEST OF DEVYN PRESS
Newly Published Bridge Books

WINNING BRIDGE INTANGIBLES
by Mike Lawrence and Keith Hanson $2.95

This book shows you how to achieve the best results possible with the knowledge you already possess. A few of the topics covered are: how to be a good partner, how to avoid giving the opponents crucial information, how to develop the best attitude at the table, and the best way to form a partnership. Recommended for: beginner through advanced.

THE FLANNERY TWO-DIAMOND CONVENTION
by Bill Flannery $7.95

Finally, a complete book on the Flannery convention, written by its creator. This teaches you the secrets to success so you will never have a misunderstanding with your partner. Included are sections on the mechanics, defenses against Flannery, the correct opening lead against the opponents' auctions, 62 example hands with explanations, and much more. Recommended for: intermediate through expert.

BRIDGE: THE BIDDER'S GAME
by Dr. George Rosenkranz $12.95

Bidding for the 80's; the concepts top experts are using today to increase their slam, game, part score, and competitive accuracy. Included are: an introduction to relays and how they can be incorporated into your present system, trump-asking and control-asking bids, new methods of cue bidding, revisions of popular conventions such as Stayman and Splinter bids, a complete update of the Romex System, with hundreds of examples. Recommended for: advanced through expert.

HAVE I GOT A STORY FOR YOU
by Patty Eber and Mike Freeman $7.95

These are humorous stories on bridge, submitted by players across the country, from the local to national level. Hundreds contributed their favorite tales; these are the best from club games, tournaments, bars and hospitality rooms. This entertaining collection is a perfect gift and is recommended for: anyone who enjoys bridge.

THE ART OF LOGICAL BIDDING
by Andrew Gorski $4.95

If you're tired of memorizing bidding sequences and still getting mediocre results at the table, this book is for you. It presents a new system, based on the inherent logic of the game. Because of the natural approach it reduces the chances of partnership misunderstandings, so you'll feel confident of reaching the best contract. Recommended for: bright beginner through intermediate.

STANDARD PLAYS OF CARD COMBINATIONS FOR CONTRACT BRIDGE by Alan Truscott,
Laura Jane Gordy, and Edward L. Gordy $5.95

Contains the 150 most important card combinations so that you can maximize your trick-taking potential. The one skill that all experts possess is the ability to handle the standard plays correctly; here is this crucial information at your fingertips. Included are plays to the opening lead, suit-handling and finesses, second hand play and third hand play. Perforated so you may remove the cards from the book if you wish. Recommended for: beginner through advanced.

THE BEST OF DEVYN PRESS
Bridge Books

A collection of the world's premier bridge authors have produced, for your enjoyment, this wide and impressive selection of books.

MATCHPOINTS
by Kit Woolsey
$9.95

The long-awaited second book by the author of the classic *Partnership Defense*. *Matchpoints* examines all of the crucial aspects of duplicate bridge. It is surprising, with the wealth of excellent books on bidding and play, how neglected matchpoint strategy has been—Kit has filled that gap forever with the best book ever written on the subject. The chapters include: general concepts, constructive bidding, competitive bidding, defensive bidding and the play.
Published October, 1982
Recommended for: intermediate through expert.
ISBN 0-910791-00-7 paperback

DYNAMIC DEFENSE
by Mike Lawrence
$9.95

One of the top authors of the '80's has produced a superior work in his latest effort. These unique hands offer you an over-the-shoulder look at how a World Champion reasons through the most difficult part of bridge. You will improve your technique as you sit at the table and attempt to find the winning sequence of plays. Each of the 65 problems is thoroughly explained and analyzed in the peerless Lawrence style.
Published October, 1982.
Recommended for: bright beginner through expert.
ISBN 0-910791-01-5 paperback

MODERN IDEAS IN BIDDING
by Dr. George Rosenkranz and Alan Truscott
$9.95

Mexico's top player combines with the bridge editor of the <u>New York Times</u> to produce a winner's guide to bidding theory. Constructive bidding, slams, pre-emptive bidding, competitive problems, overcalls and many other valuable concepts are covered in depth. Increase your accuracy with the proven methods which have won numerous National titles and have been adopted by a diverse group of champions.
Published October, 1982
Recommended for: intermediate through expert.
ISBN 0-910791-02-3 paperback

THE COMPLETE BOOK OF OPENING LEADS
by Easley Blackwood
$12.95

An impressive combination: the most famous name in bridge has compiled the most comprehensive book ever written on opening leads. Almost every situation imaginable is presented with a wealth of examples from world championship play. Learn to turn your wild guesses into intelligent thrusts at the enemy declarer by using all the available information. Chapters include when to lead long suits, dangerous opening leads, leads against slam contracts, doubling for a lead, when to lead partner's suit, and many others.
Published November, 1982.
Recommended for: beginner through advanced.
ISBN 0-910791-05-8 paperback

THE BEST OF DEVYN PRESS
Bridge Books

A collection of the world's premier bridge authors have produced, for your enjoyment, this wide and impressive selection of books.

TEST YOUR PLAY AS DECLARER, VOLUME 2
by Jeff Rubens and Paul Lukacs
$5.95

Two celebrated authors have collaborated on 100 challenging and instructive problems which are sure to sharpen your play. Each hand emphasizes a different principle in how declarer should handle his cards. These difficult exercises will enable you to profit from your errors and enjoy learning at the same time.
Published October, 1982.
Recommended for: intermediate through expert.
ISBN 0-910791-03-1 paperback

TABLE TALK
by Jude Goodwin
$5.95

This collection of cartoons is a joy to behold. What Snoopy did for dogs and Garfield did for cats, Sue and her gang does for bridge players. If you want a realistic, humorous view of the clubs and tournaments you attend, this will brighten your day. You'll meet the novices, experts, obnoxious know-it-alls, bridge addicts and other characters who inhabit that fascinating subculture known as the bridge world.
Recommended for: all bridge players.
ISBN 0-910891-04-X paperback

THE CHAMPIONSHIP BRIDGE SERIES

In-depth discussions of the mostly widely used conventions...how to play them, when to use them and how to defend against them. The solution for those costly partnership misunderstandings. Each of these pamphlets is written by one of the world's top experts. **Recommended for: beginner through advanced.**
95 ¢ each, Any 12 for $9.95, All 24 for $17.90

VOLUME I [#1-12]
PUBLISHED 1980

1. Popular Conventions by Randy Baron
2. The Blackwood Convention by Easley Blackwood
3. The Stayman Convention by Paul Soloway
4. Jacoby Transfer Bids by Oswald Jacoby
5. Negative Doubles by Alvin Roth
6. Weak Two Bids by Howard Schenken
7. Defense Against Strong Club Openings by Kathy Wei
8. Killing Their No Trump by Ron Andersen
9. Splinter Bids by Andrew Bernstein
10. Michaels' Cue Bid by Mike Passell
11. The Unusual No Trump by Alvin Roth
12. Opening Leads by Robert Ewen

VOLUME II [#13-24]
PUBLISHED 1981

13. More Popular Conventions by Randy Baron
14. Major Suit Raises by Oswald Jacoby
15. Swiss Team Tactics by Carol & Tom Sanders
16. Match Point Tactics by Ron Andersen
17. Overcalls by Mike Lawrence
18. Balancing by Mike Lawrence
19. The Weak No Trump by Judi Radin
20. One No Trump Forcing by Alan Sontag
21. Flannery by William Flannery
22. Drury by Kerri Shuman
23. Doubles by Bobby Goldman
24. Opening Preempts by Bob Hamman

THE BEST OF DEVYN PRESS

Bridge Conventions Complete
by Amalya Kearse
$17.95

An undated and expanded edition (over 800 pages) of the reference book no duplicate player can afford to be without. The reviews say it all:

"At last! A book with both use and appeal for expert or novice plus everybody in between. Every partnership will find material they will wish to add to their present system. Not only are all the conventions in use anywhere today clearly and aptly described, but Kearse criticizes various treatments regarding potential flaws and how they can be circumvented.

"Do yourself a favor and add this book to your shelf even if you don't enjoy most bridge books. This book is a treat as well as a classic."
—ACBL BULLETIN

"A must for duplicate fans, this is a comprehensive, well-written guide through the maze of systems and conventions. This should be particularly useful to those who don't want to be taken off guard by an unfamiliar convention, because previously it would have been necessary to amass several references to obtain all the information presented."
—BRIDGE WORLD MAGAZINE

Published January, 1984

Recommended for: all duplicate players

ISBN 0-910791-07-4 paperback

Test Your Play As Declarer, Volume 1
by Jeff Rubens and Paul Lukacs
$5.95

Any reader who studies this book carefully will certainly become much more adept at playing out a hand. There are 89 hands here, each emphasizing a particular point in declarer play. The solution to each problem explains how and why a declarer should handle his hands in a certain way. A reprint of the original.

Published December, 1983

Recommended for: intermediate through expert

ISBN 0-910791-12-0 paperback

Devyn Press Book of Partnership Understandings
by Mike Lawrence
$2.95

Stop bidding misunderstandings before they occur with this valuable guide. It covers all the significant points you should discuss with your partner, whether you are forming a new partnership or you have played together for years.

Published December, 1983

Recommended for: novice through expert

ISBN 0-910791-08-2 paperback

101 Bridge Maxims
by H. W. Kelsey
$7.95

The experience of a master player and writer condensed into 101 easy-to-understand adages. Each hand will help you remember these essential rules during the heat of battle.

Published December, 1983

Recommended for: bright beginner through advanced.

ISBN 0-910791-10-4 paperback

Play Bridge with Mike Lawrence
by Mike Lawrence
$9.95

Follow Mike through a 2-session matchpoint event at a regional tournament, and learn how to gather information from the auction, the play of the cards and the atmosphere at the table. When to go against the field, compete, make close doubles, and more.

Published December, 1983

Recommended for: bright beginner through expert.

ISBN 0-910791-09-0 paperback

Play These Hands With Me
by Terence Reese
$7.95

Studies 60 hands in minute detail. How to analyze your position and sum up information you have available, with a post-mortem reviewing main points.

Published December, 1983

Recommended for: intermediate through expert.

ISBN 0-910791-11-2 paperback

THE BEST OF DEVYN PRESS ♣

DEVYN PRESS BOOK OF BRIDGE PUZZLES #1, #2, and #3
by Alfred Sheinwold
$4.95 each

Each of the three books in this series is part of the most popular and entertaining collection of bridge problems ever written. They were originally titled "Pocket Books of Bridge Puzzles #1, #2, and #3." The 90 hands in each volume are practical and enjoyable—the kind that you attempt to solve every time you play. They also make perfect gifts for your friends, whether they are inexperienced novices or skilled masters.

Published January, 1981. Paperback

Recommended for: beginner through advanced.

TICKETS TO THE DEVIL
by Richard Powell $5.95

This is the most popular bridge novel ever written by the author of Woody Allen's "Bananas," "The Young Philadelphians," and Elvis Presley's "Follow That Dream."

Tickets has a cast of characters ranging from the Kings and Queens of tournament bridge down to the deuces. Among them are:

Ace McKinley, famous bridge columnist who needs a big win to restore his fading reputation.

Carole Clark, who lost a husband because she led a singleton king.

Bubba Worthington, young socialite who seeks the rank of Life Master to prove his virility.

The Dukes and the Ashcrafts, who have partnership troubles in bridge and in bed.

Tony Manuto, who plays for pay, and handles cards as if they were knives.

Powell shuffles these and many other players to deal out comedy, violence and drama in a perfect mixture.

Published 1979. . . Paperback
Recommended for: all bridge players.

PARTNERSHIP DEFENSE
by Kit Woolsey
$8.95

Kit's first book is unanimously considered THE classic defensive text so that you can learn the secrets of the experts. It contains a detailed discussion of attitude, count, and suit-preference signals; leads; matchpoints; defensive conventions; protecting partner; with quizzes and a unique partnership test at the end.

Alan Truscott, Bridge Editor, New York Times: The best new book to appear in 1980 seems certain to be "Partnership Defense in Bridge."

The author has surveyed a complex and vital field that has been largely neglected in the literature of the game. The player of moderate experience is sure to benefit from the wealth of examples and problems dealing with signaling and other matters relating to cooperation in defense.

And experts who feel they have nothing more to learn neglect this book at their peril: The final test of 20 problems has been presented to some of the country's best partnerships, and non has approached a maximum score.

Bridge World Magazine: As a practical guide for tournament players, no defensive book compares with Kit Woolsey's "Partnership Defense in Bridge" which is by far the best book of its kind that we have seen. As a technical work it is superb, and any good player who does not read it will be making one of his biggest errors of bridge judgment.

The author's theme is partnership cooperation. He believes there are many more points to be won through careful play, backed by relatively complete understandings, than through spectacular coups or even through choices among sensible conventions. We agree. If you don't, you will very likely change your mind (or at least modify the strength of your opinion) after reading what Woolsey has to say.

Published 1980. . . Paperback
Recommended for: Intermediate through expert.

DO YOU KNOW YOUR PARTNER? by Andy Bernstein and Randy Baron $1.95 A fun-filled quiz to allow you to really get to know your partner. Some questions concern bridge, some don't — only you can answer and only your partner can score it. An inexpensive way to laugh yourself to a better partnership.

Published 1979   paperback
Recommended for: all bridge players.

DEVYN PRESS
151 Thierman Lane
Louisville, KY 40207
(502) 895-1354

OUTSIDE KY. CALL TOLL FREE
1-800-626-1598
FOR VISA / MASTER CARD
ORDERS ONLY

ORDER FORM

Number
Wanted

DO YOU KNOW YOUR PARTNER?, Bernstein-Baron	x $ 1.95 =
COMPLETE BOOK OF OPENING LEADS, Blackwood	x 12.95 =
HAVE I GOT A STORY FOR YOU!, Eber and Freeman	x 7.95 =
THE FLANNERY TWO DIAMOND CONVENTION, Flannery	x 7.95 =
TABLE TALK, Goodwin	x 5.95 =
THE ART OF LOGICAL BIDDING, Gorski	x 4.95 =
INDIVIDUAL CHAMPIONSHIP BRIDGE SERIES (Please specify)	x .95 =
BRIDGE CONVENTIONS COMPLETE, Kearse (Paperback)	x 17.95 =
BRIDGE CONVENTIONS COMPLETE, Kearse (Hardcover)	x 24.95 =
101 BRIDGE MAXIMS, Kelsey	x 7.95 =
DYNAMIC DEFENSE, Lawrence	x 9.95 =
PARTNERSHIP UNDERSTANDINGS, Lawrence	x 2.95 =
PLAY BRIDGE WITH MIKE LAWRENCE, Lawrence	x 9.95 =
WINNING BRIDGE INTANGIBLES, Lawrence and Hanson	x 2.95 =
TICKETS TO THE DEVIL, Powell	x 5.95 =
PLAY THESE HANDS WITH ME, Reese	x 7.95 =
BRIDGE: THE BIDDER'S GAME, Rosenkranz	x 12.95 =
MODERN IDEAS IN BIDDING, Rosenkranz-Truscott	x 9.95 =
TEST YOUR PLAY AS DECLARER, VOL. 1, Rubens-Lukacs	x 5.95 =
TEST YOUR PLAY AS DECLARER, VOL. 2, Rubens-Lukacs	x 5.95 =
DEVYN PRESS BOOK OF BRIDGE PUZZLES #1, Sheinwold	x 4.95 =
DEVYN PRESS BOOK OF BRIDGE PUZZLES #2, Sheinwold	x 4.95 =
DEVYN PRESS BOOK OF BRIDGE PUZZLES, # 3, Sheinwold	x 4.95 =
STANDARD PLAYS OF CARD COMBINATIONS FOR CONTRACT	
BRIDGE, Truscott, Gordy and Gordy	x 5.95 =
PARTNERSHIP DEFENSE, Woolsey	x 8.95 =
MATCHPOINTS, Woolsey	x 9.95 =

QUANTITY DISCOUNT
ON ABOVE ITEMS:
10% over $25, 20% over $50

We accept checks, money
orders and VISA or MASTER
CARD. For charge card
orders, send your card number and expiration date.

SUBTOTAL [   ]

LESS QUANTITY DISCOUNT
TOTAL [   ]

THE CHAMPIONSHIP BRIDGE SERIES
VOLUME 1 .... x $9.95 (No further discount) [   ]
THE CHAMPIONSHIP BRIDGE SERIES
VOLUME II .... x 9.95 (No further discount) [   ]
ALL 24 OF THE CHAMPIONSHIP
BRIDGE SERIES .... x 17.90 (No further discount) [   ]

ADD $1.00   TOTAL FOR BOOKS [   ]
SHIPPING   SHIPPING ALLOWANCE [   ]
PER ORDER   AMOUNT ENCLOSED [   ]

NAME _____

ADDRESS _____

CITY _____ STATE _____ ZIP _____